LAURA HENNE

# Dive In!

## A Topsy-Turvy-Say-It-Out-Loud
# UNDERWATER ADVENTURE

Written by

Recess Monkey

Illustrated by

Rob McClurkan

Oh, hello there, you startled me!
I'm Sir Sebastian Stockingbottomham.

Yes, *that* Sir Sebastian
Stockingbottomham—
the famous undersea explorer.

Today...

# We are going on an adventure!

You know, that wasn't quite exciting enough.
Can you help me?

*Yell it* with me now, as *loudly* as you can:

# Today We ARE Going ON AN ADVENTURE!

*Ooooooh*, I like that! Perfect.

Now, if you're going
to dive like an
undersea explorer,
you've got to *sound* like
an undersea explorer...
and I know a little trick!

Put your finger between your lips and move it up and down,
and then say these words like *you* are underwater:

Saltwater

Oh, yes! That's nice! *More!*

Jellyfish

You're really getting the hang of it now!

Clam chowder

Yes! Yes! That sounds just right.

Amazing! When you see words like this
now you know what to do!

# Let's dive in!

I'll count to ten and
you'll hold your breath.

Ready then?

I'm *serious*! You've got
to hold your breath
until I get all
the way to ten.

Deep breath in...
and, go!

1 2 3

Look, may I take this moment to say that you are doing
a wonderful job so far? What's that? *Keep* counting?
Ah yes. So sorry.

4 5 6

I've *never* seen such talented breath holding in all my days—
what's that? Sorry, I do get carried away.

7 8 9 10

*Hooray!* We've made it!
But I will warn you, the ocean floor is host
to all kinds of mysterious animals.

Undersea explorers, this... is Burton.

**Burt.**

Ah yes. Sorry. Burt.
Say hello to Burt the Blobfish.
Just look at him there.
Can't you tell he's ready
for an adventure of a lifetime?

**NO I'm not.**

Um, that doesn't really sound
as exciting as I'd hoped, Burt.

I think Burt needs a little help.

He just seems a little... um... *flat.*

How about we give him a little "pep,"

as they say. Let's tickle him.

Go on, then. Tickle him with your finger!

Let's see if we can help him be more energetic.

Tickle, Tickle, Tickle!

# Hook, line, and sinker!

He did it! Look at that posture of yours, Burt!
That's more like a fish who gets things done.

Oh, by no means are we done, Burt!
We're just getting *started*!

**we're done?**

Our hero, Burt, needs help.
He looks too comfortable!

Let's give him a gentle nudge
with our fingers
to get him on his way!

*Ready?*

PUUUUUUSH!

Did you *see* that?! He's really moving now.
The adventure of a lifetime!

He's ready for a *bigger* push now.

What do you say we tilt the book down
a little to help him pick up some steam?
That'll get him moving!

Ready, then?
On your marks,
get set, and...

TILT

DOWN

Success!

Oh, but where is he?

He forgot to tell us where he was going!

Let's find him! Hmmm...

Can you look under where you are

sitting? Go ahead, stand up.

Is he there? There on the cushion?

No?

Look under your foot. Not there either?

Oh. I'm worried now. We should call for him.
All together now, let's call his name!

# Burt the Blobfish!

That didn't work... Try it even louder!

# Burt the Blobfish!

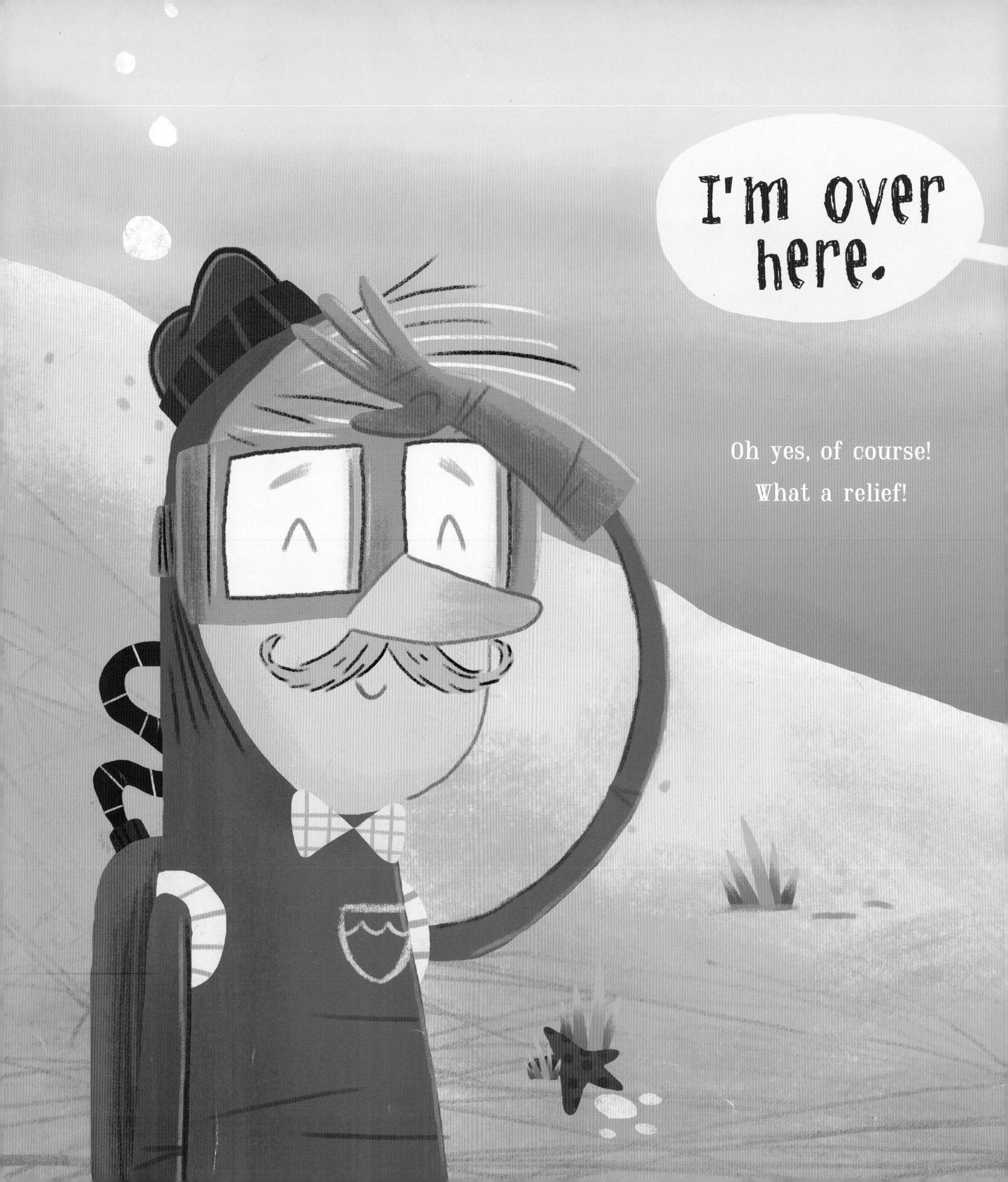


Oh yes, of course!
What a relief!

He just rolled off the page,
that rascal!

We must turn the book back the other way!
All together now!

TILT UP

Why there he is!
Welcome back, Burt!
Tell us about where you went!

But first, I'm sorry,
is that a *hat*?

Yes, yes, the best adventures are shared in friendship! Good for you, Burton! Friendship as deep as the ocean! Our hero has found a traveling buddy! Now we're cooking! And that's nature for you! The web of life! The balance of animals and friendship.

The blah blah blah...

Psst.
Hey. You.
YES, YOU. COME CLOSER.
It's okay, he can't hear us.
WE'VE BEEN TALKING, KID, AND WE NEED YOUR HELP.
We need to shake up this "adventure."
TAKE THE BOOK AND SHAKE IT REALLY HARD.
Trust us. It's for the best.
SHAKE IT. NOW.

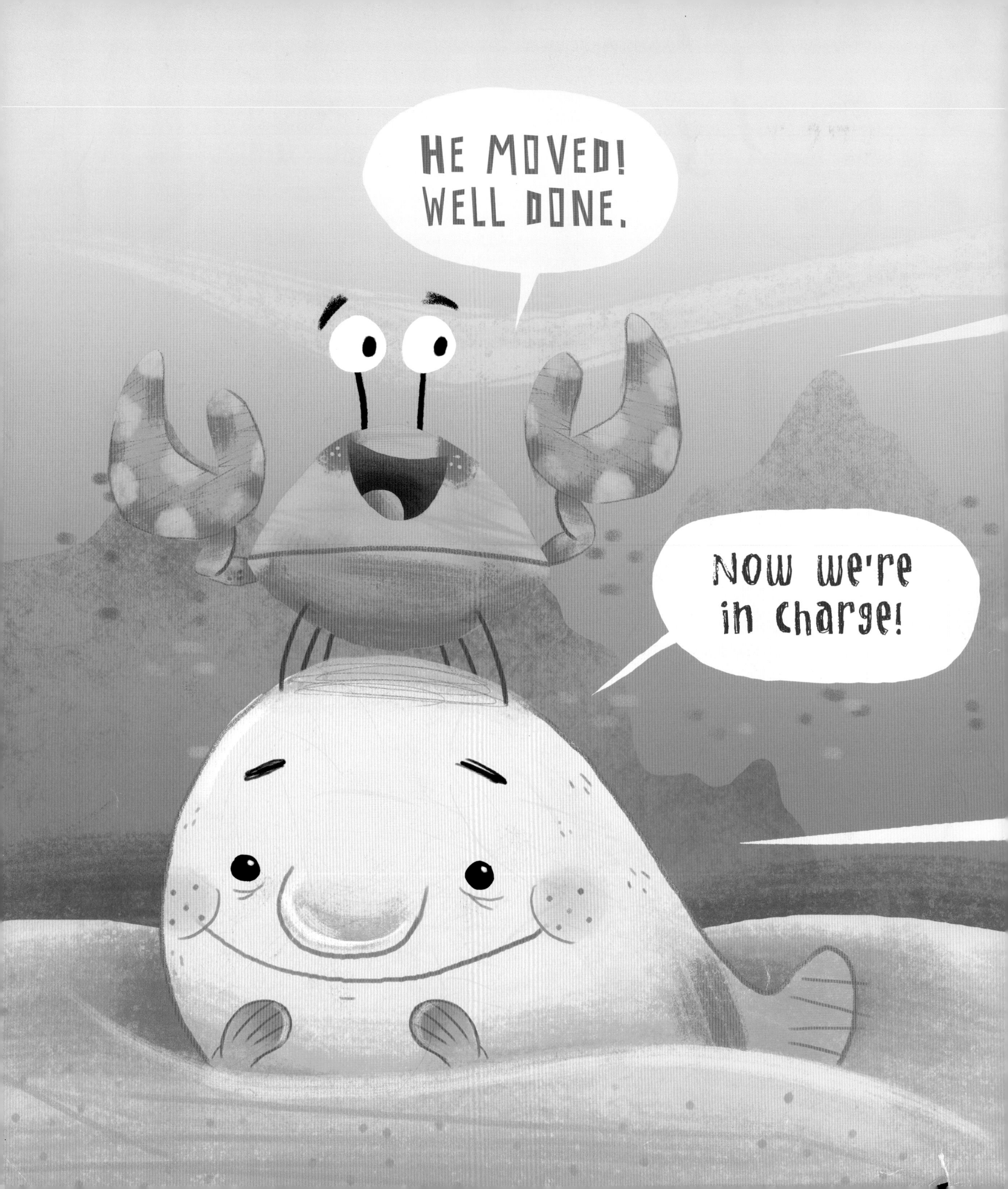
HE MOVED! WELL DONE.
Now we're in charge!

LET'S TICKLE HIM.
YES. HE NEEDS A LITTLE "PEP!"
Crab, can you make that more exciting? Say it like you're underwater.
YES. HE NEEDS A LITTLE "PEP!"
That's perfect! Now go on, underwater explorer. Tickle him!
"TICKLE, TICKLE, TICKLE!"
No, please! I'm very ticklish under my armpits!

I like where this is heading.
ALL HE NEEDS NOW IS A STRONG BREEZE TO GET BACK TO SHORE.
BlOW on him as hard as you can.
HARDER!

Oof!

WHAT AN ADVENTURE!

Well that's nature for you, always surprising
you when you least expect it!

TURN BACK AROUND

Now, okay, sure, it *looks* like I've just been tossed onto
the sand by a couple of sneaky sea creatures…
but I assure you this was my plan all along.

Really. I am a famous explorer, after all.
And, like they always say, you're in good hands
with Sir Sebastian Stockingbottomham!

Wait, they don't always say that? They *should* say that!

In any case,
I'm so thrilled you
came along on this
underwater odyssey!

See you next time,
explorer!

## About the Authors

Recess Monkey's Drew Holloway and Jack Forman (pictured below) met as teachers at the same Seattle elementary school and have been laughing ever since. Their Recess Monkey album *Deep Sea Diver* is propelled by undersea rhythms and jokes as ridiculous as the ones in this book. Find out more about them and their music at recessmonkey.com!

## About the Illustrator

Rob McClurkan is an author and illustrator who enjoys bringing colorful characters to life. Although he's never seen a blobfish in real life, he often feels like one after he's eaten too many gummy worms. Rob lives near Atlanta, Georgia, with his wife, two kids, and their dog Izzi, who has the amazing superpower of shedding on everything. To see more of Rob's illustration work and books, visit seerobdraw.com!

I'm sorry,
I seem to have
lost my keys.
Has anyone
seen my keys?

With special thanks to the entire Compendium family.

CREDITS:
Written by: Jack Forman & Drew Holloway
Illustrated by: Rob McClurkan
Designed by: Megan Gandt Guansing
Edited by: Amelia Riedler

Library of Congress: 2016945884
ISBN: 978-1-943200-13-9

1st printing. Printed in China with soy inks. A021609001